Another Sommer-Time Story™

Your Job Is Easy

by Carl Sommer
Illustrated by Kennon James

Advance
PUBLISHING, INC.

Permissions
Advance Publishing, Inc.
6950 Fulton St.
Houston, TX 77022

www.advancepublishing.com

First Edition
Printed in Singapore

Library of Congress Cataloging-in-Publication Data

Sommer, Carl, 1930-
  Your Job is Easy/by Carl Sommer; illustrated by Kennon James.--1st ed.
    p. cm. -- (Another Sommer-Time Story)
  Summary: When a mother and father exchange jobs for a day, they each come to respect the value of what the other does.
    Cover title: Carl Sommer's Your Job is Easy.
    ISBN 1-57537-018-2 (hardcover: alk. paper). -- ISBN 1-57537-067-0 (library binding: alk. paper)
    [1. Farm life Fiction. 2. Family life Fiction. 3. Work Fiction.]
I. James, Kennon, ill. II. Title. III. Title: Carl Sommer's Your Job is Easy. IV. Series: Sommer, Carl, 1930- Another Sommer-Time Story.
PZ7.S696235Ya 2000   99-16376
[E]--dc21   CIP

Another Sommer-Time Story™

Your Job Is Easy

Sam and Jane lived on a farm with their children, Billy, Susie, and Baby Timmy. Taking care of the farm was hard work, but they loved it anyway.

For them, life had always been peaceful and pleasant—that is, until today.

The problem began when Jane looked at the newly plowed fields and asked, "Sam, why do you plow the rows so crookedly?"

"What difference does it make," answered Sam, "if the rows are perfectly straight or a little crooked?"

"Well," said Jane, "if you're going to plow, you might as well do it right."

"It's not as easy as you think," said Sam.

"Come on!" laughed Jane. "How hard can it be to plow a straight line?"

"Well," grumbled Sam, "if you think it's so easy, why don't *you* try it? You'll see how hard it is."

"I'd love to," said Jane with a big smile. "But then who would do my chores?"

"I will!" chuckled Sam. "Your job is easy."

Jane put her hands on her hips. "If you really think my job is easy, let's switch jobs. I'd love to have your e-a-s-y job!"

"Great!" said Sam. "We'll start tomorrow!"

When Sam and Jane went to sleep that night, they had many happy thoughts about the next day.

Because they thought their work would be so easy, they dreamed of all the fun things they would do with their spare time.

In the middle of the night, little Timmy became hungry and began to cry, "Wahhhhh!"

Sam was sound asleep. Jane poked Sam in the ribs, and called sweetly, "Sam!"

Sam grunted and rolled over.

"Oh, S-a-a-a-m," she called louder. "The baby's crying, and today—you're the mama."

Then Jane rolled over and went happily back to sleep.

Sam had not planned for this. He stumbled out of bed and put some milk in the baby's bottle. Then he heated the bottle and sat down to feed little Timmy.

"Ringgggg!!!"

Sam had just crawled back into bed when the alarm went off. "Oh, nooooo!" he groaned.

"Oh, yesssss!" shouted Jane as she leaped out of bed.

While getting dressed, Jane smiled and said, "This is going to be such an e-a-s-y day."

She skipped off to the shed and began to whistle a happy tune. As she passed by the vegetable garden, she put on the sprinkler system.

Jane had the whole day planned. She was going to work smarter, not harder! Jane said to herself, "Sam always carries the heavy buckets to feed the animals. But I have a much better idea—I'll use the tractor!"

Jane rode the tractor for a short distance, and then it stopped. She cranked the engine, but it would not start. She cranked and cranked some more.

By the time she thought to check the gas, the battery had run down.

By now Jane was behind in her chores, and the cow was very unhappy about it. Jane hurriedly milked the cow, and then rushed to get a battery from the truck and a can of gas.

Switching batteries was not easy. But after getting another battery and a tank full of gas, the tractor roared to life.

Now the goats and pigs and chickens were yelling for food.

"Oh my!" said Jane. "Those animals are really impatient!"

Jane loaded the food onto the trailer, and then ran to fill the pails with water.

Meanwhile, Billy and Susie were ready for breakfast. Since Sam had spent so much of the night awake with Baby Timmy, he was having a hard time getting out of bed.

Billy and Susie began bouncing on the bed and yelling, "Get up, Daddy! We're hungry."

"Okay! Okay!" mumbled Sam. "I'm getting up."

As he put on his robe, he said, "I'll have plenty of free time today. I'll just take a nap this afternoon."

Sam walked into the kitchen and proudly announced, "Today, Daddy is going to make everyone an extra special breakfast."

Sam began to whistle. "This is going to be such an e-a-s-y day," he said to himself as he cracked the eggs.

Just as Sam started toward the stove, Rover spotted Kitty. In a flash, Rover and Kitty dashed across the floor—right between Sam's legs!

"Oops!" yelled Sam as he tried to dodge the playful pets. But he slipped, and the bowl of eggs went flying out of his hands! Eggs flew everywhere.

"Oh nooooo!" yelled Sam. "I'd better clean up this mess fast." As he picked up the mop, Baby Timmy began to cry.

"The children really need to be fed first," he muttered to himself. "I'll clean up the floor later."

"Instead of eggs," he said to Billy and Susie, "I'll make you some oatmeal. It will be ready in no time."

As Sam hurried to get the oatmeal, he forgot about the eggs on the floor. "Swooshhhh!" He stepped into the gooey mess and slid right into the kitchen cabinet, banging his nose!

"Oh, my nose! My nose!" he cried as he searched for a bandage.

After bandaging his nose, Sam put the oatmeal on the stove. "While the oatmeal cooks," he said, "I'll go and clean the floor."

As Sam began to clean the floor, he said, "Oh my! These eggs are very sticky. I need to get a pail of water."

Meanwhile, Jane had come to the house to fill the water buckets for the thirsty animals. But just as she had turned the faucet on outside, Sam had turned the faucet on in the basement. With the sprinkler system on and both faucets running, water came out slowly.

While Sam was waiting for the pail to fill up with water, he heard Billy scream, "Daddy, there's smoke in the kitchen!"

"Oh, no!" yelled Sam. "The oatmeal!"

He raced upstairs—but he was too late.

"What a mess! What a mess!" groaned Sam as he saw oatmeal bubbling onto the stove. He quickly opened all the windows to let the smoke clear out.

The children cried louder, "Daddy! We're hungry!"

Sam reached for a loaf of bread. "I'll make you peanut butter sandwiches."

After feeding all the children, Sam looked at the messy stove. "I need to get a bucket of water to clean this up."

Suddenly it hit him. "Water? Oh no! I forgot to turn off the faucet downstairs!"

Sam raced to the basement, but he was too late. Jane had turned off the sprinkler system and the outside faucet. Now water inside was coming out full force! The basement was flooded!

"What a mess! What a mess!" groaned Sam as he sloshed through the water. "Why is it that *everything* I do is wrong?"

Outside, Jane had the trailer loaded and was
on her way to feed the hungry animals. They
were making such an uproar that Jane drove the
tractor fast—much too fast over the rocky road.
Suddenly, a wheel hit a rock, and the trailer
overturned, spilling everything onto the road.

"Oh my!" she cried. "What am I going to do?"

She sat there thinking. Suddenly she jumped
up and said, "I have a great idea! I'll let Mama
Pig eat the food off the ground."

Jane hurried to the pigpen and tied a rope around Mama Pig. With the rope securely tied around one hand, Jane opened the gate with the other. But when Mama Pig saw the food, she bolted through the open gate.

Jane tried to hold her back, but the pig was much stronger. Jane slipped, and Mama Pig dragged her through the mud—on her face! The baby pigs tagged happily along.

Mama Pig did not stop running until she came to the food.

"Oh, my nose! My nose!" cried Jane.

Jane went to the shed to get a bandage for her nose. She washed herself as well as she could, and then ran back to put the pigs into their pen.

"Here piggy, piggy, piggy!" Jane yelled. But the baby pigs did not want to go back to their pen. They were having too much fun running around the farm.

Meanwhile, the goats and chickens were yelling louder than ever for their food.

Jane finally enticed Mama Pig into the pen with more food. But she had to chase the squealing piglets all over the farm.

Jane was exhausted from chasing the baby pigs and carrying them to the pen. Then she went and fed all the rest of the animals.

"Whew!" sighed Jane. "Am I glad that's done! That was a lot of work."

Now she was very hot—and very tired. No longer did she whistle.

The whistling had also stopped in the house. Sam was busy scooping pails of water from the flooded basement.

And when he spotted clothes that needed to be washed, dried, and ironed, he became even more depressed. He shook his head and groaned, "How will I *ever* get everything done?"

By now it was lunchtime.

The children called, "Daddy, we're hungry."

"But I just fed you!" complained Sam.

Sam had worked hard the whole morning, but nothing was finished. The dishes were dirty, the stove was caked with burnt oatmeal, and the floor was covered with eggs. Worst of all, the

basement was still under water.

Sam had planned to prepare a special lunch, but now all he wanted was to make something very quick and very easy.

"I'm going to feed you cold cereal and milk," said Sam, wiping his brow. "Daddy has a lot of work to do."

With all the animals happy and full, things in the field began to settle down. Jane walked over to the tractor and smiled, "Now *I'll* show Sam how to plow!"

All day long Jane had been looking forward to plowing the field. Now she could relax on the tractor and prove once and for all how easy it was to plow a straight line.

Jane looked behind her to make sure she was going straight. She was doing a pretty good job—that is, until the tractor began to slow down.

Jane looked down and saw that she had driven the tractor right into a large mud puddle. Jane pushed harder on the gas pedal, but the tires only spun in the mud. And the more she pushed on the gas pedal, the deeper the tractor sank into the mud.

She was stuck!

"Now what should I do?" she groaned.

Jane thought and thought. Then she remembered the mule. "Manny! He can help me pull out the tractor."

Jane trudged through the mud to get the mule. But stubborn Manny would not come.

Jane hollered and pushed and tugged—but Manny refused to budge.

Then a thought flashed through her mind. "That's it!" she said. "I'll fill a bucket with Manny's favorite food—carrots."

When Manny saw the carrots, he jumped up and followed Jane to the tractor.

Jane tied Manny to the tractor. He pulled, but the tractor would not move.

"I have a great idea!" thought Jane. "I'll get a longer rope so Manny can get a running start."

She went to the barn and found an old rope. "Oh good!" she said. "This should get the tractor out of the mud."

Jane hurried back with the longer rope. She again tied Manny to the tractor and put the carrots out in front of him.

Then Jane pulled on the rope as hard as she could and yelled, "Go, Manny! Go!"

Manny leaped up and raced for the carrots. He ran so fast that the rope *snapped!* Before Jane knew it, she was yanked off her feet and dragged through the mud on her face.

"That's it!" said Jane, shaking her head and spitting out mud. "I'm going home! I don't care if the field is crooked or straight! This has been the hardest day of my life!"

She left the mule in the field and the tractor in the mud. Then she slowly trudged home.

Back home, Sam was toiling in the basement, mopping up water. He was tired, his nose hurt, his back ached, and the house was a big mess.

Sam shook his head and groaned, "Ohhhhh! This has been the hardest day of my life!"

Just then, the kids screamed, "Daddy!"

"Oh nooooo!" cried Sam. "What now?"

"It's Mommy!" yelled the children as they jumped up and down. "Mommy is home!"

Sam ran upstairs to meet her.

When Jane entered the house, she stood there in amazement. She saw burnt oatmeal on the stove, dried eggs on the floor, and dirty dishes everywhere. Then she saw raggedy Sam and his bandaged nose.

Sam looked at Jane—first at her tangled hair, next at her muddy clothes, and then at her bandaged nose. Finally he peeked outside and saw the tractor stuck in the mud.

Jane began to chuckle, and so did Sam. Soon they were bending over from laughing so hard.

When they told each other what had happened, they started all over again—laughing and laughing some more!

Finally, Sam gave Jane a hug and apologized. "I'm sorry for what I said. I've learned my lesson. I'll *never* again say that your job is easy."

Jane gave Sam a kiss and said, "I'm also sorry for what I said. The work you do *sure* isn't easy!"

Jane happily went back to *her* job—which pleased the kids. Sam gladly went back to *his* job—which pleased the animals.

Life went back to being peaceful and pleasant. And *that* pleased everyone!

Read Exciting Character-Building Adventures
★★★ Another Sommer-Time Stories ★★★

Available as Read-Alongs on CDs or Cassettes

Visit www.AdvancePublishing.com
For Additional Character-Building Resources